TEEN TITANS GO!™

FOOD FRIGHT AND PAR FOR THE COURSE

Raintree is an imprint of Capstone Global Library Limited, a company incorporated in England and Wales having its
registered office at 264 Banbury Road, Oxford, OX2 7DY – Registered company number: 6695582

www.raintree.co.uk
myorders@raintree.co.uk

Edited by Chris Harbo
Designed by Brann Garvey and Hilary Wacholz
Production by Kathy McColley
Originated by Capstone Global Library Ltd
Printed and bound in India

ISBN 978 1 4747 7322 5
22 21 20 19 18
10 9 8 7 6 5 4 3 2 1

British Library Cataloguing in Publication Data
A full catalogue record for this book is available from the British Library.

TEEN TITANS GO!™

SHOLLY FISCH   MERRILL HAGAN
WRITERS

BEN BATES   JORGE CORONA
ARTISTS

JEREMY LAWSON
COLOURIST

WES ABBOTT
LETTERER

DAN HIPP
COVER ARTIST

raintree 🍃

a Capstone company — publishers for children

SANDWICH TIME, SANDWICH TIME!

THERE'S NO TIME LIKE SANDWICH TIME

GREASE the COOK

EXCEPT FOR MAYBE CORN DOG TIME OR BATTERED, DEEP-FRIED CHOCOLATE TI--

AAAAAAAAAAGGGGHHHH!

"FOOD FRIGHT"

WRITTEN BY
SHOLLY FISCH

ART BY
BEN BATES

LETTERS BY
WES ABBOTT

PIZZ

--MY SANDWICH!

I DIDN'T DO IT!

DID YOU STUB THE TOE AGAIN?

WHY DOES THIS KEEP HAPPENING TO ME?

WHY? WHY? WHY?!

THE QUESTION ISN'T "WHY," IT'S "HOW." HOW DID SOMEONE GET INTO THE FRIDGE WITHOUT OPENING IT?

MAYBE THERE'S A CLUE INSIDE--

YEAH, THAT LOOKS LIKE A CLUE.

PIZZA MONSTER!

YOU LEFT THIS IN OUR *FRIDGE?* WHAT *IS* THIS THING?

LEFTOVERS.

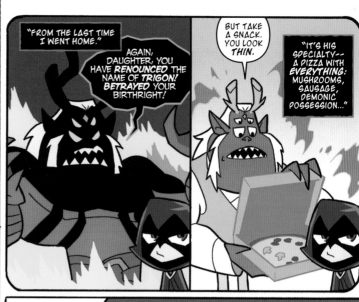

"FROM THE LAST TIME I WENT HOME."

AGAIN, DAUGHTER, YOU HAVE *RENOUNCED* THE NAME OF *TRIGON!* *BETRAYED* YOUR BIRTHRIGHT!

BUT TAKE A SNACK. YOU LOOK *THIN.*

"IT'S HIS SPECIALTY-- A PIZZA WITH *EVERYTHING:* MUSHROOMS, SAUSAGE, DEMONIC POSSESSION..."

DEMONIC POSSESSION ?!!!

IT BEATS *PINEAPPLE.*

HOW DOES ONE DEFEAT THE *DEMON-INFESTED* PIZZA?

DEMON-INFESTED *PIZZA CUTTER?*

OR WE COULD TRY...

...THIS!

THAT CREATURE KEPT EATING CYBORG'S *SANDWICHES,* BUT NOT STARFIRE'S *CAKE.* WHY NOT?

BECAUSE DEMONIC PIZZA MONSTERS FROM THE UNDERWORLD CAN'T STAND--

--ANGEL FOOD CAKE!

"PAR FOR THE COURSE"

WRITTEN BY
MERRILL HAGAN

ART BY
JORGE CORONA

COLOR BY
JEREMY LAWSON

LETTERS BY
WES ABBOTT

COVER BY
DAN HIPP

EDITED BY
ALEX ANTONE

THAT'S IT! YOU'RE GOING DOWN!

WHOA, DUDE! WHAT ARE YOU ATTACKING ME FOR?

THERE'S NO WAY YOU GOT THAT HOLE-IN-ONE ON YOUR OWN!

ROBIN! ARE YOU ACCUSING ME OF CHEATING?

"YOUR SHOT WAS NOWHERE NEAR THE HOLE!

"BUT THEN YOU TURNED INTO A PTERODACTYL AND FLAPPED YOUR WINGS AND BLEW THE BALL RIGHT IN FOR THE HOLE-IN-ONE!"

YOU **TOTALLY** CHEATED!

I GET IT, BRO. YOU'RE JUST UPSET BECAUSE YOU KNOW I'M ONE STEP CLOSER TO WINNING THE BET! BECAUSE WHEN I WIN...

...I GET YOUR CAPE!

"THERE ARE JUST SO MANY POSSIBILITIES, ROBIN...

"I COULD USE IT AS A TOWEL!

"OR MAYBE FOR A HOTLY ANTICIPATED COSTUME UPDATE!

"NAH--I'LL PROBABLY JUST CUT IT INTO PIECES AND USE IT AS CONFETTI TO CELEBRATE THE NEXT TIME SPEEDY DOES SOMETHING BETTER THAN YOU!"

NO WAY, BEAST BOY! YOU'RE JUST CHEATING BECAUSE OF THE BET YOU MADE! BECAUSE WHEN I WIN...

...I GET TO TURN YOUR ROOM INTO MY DOJO!

BUT DON'T WORRY-- I'VE GOT A DOG CRATE WITH YOUR NAME ON IT.

"DUDE! DON'T EVEN JOKE ABOUT CRATING ME! I SLEPT IN ONE WHILE I WAS BEING POTTY TRAINED...

...SO MANY DARK MEMORIES...

WELL, REGARDLESS, MY CAPE IS SAFE!

IT'S JUST A CAPE, ROBIN...WHAT DO YOU CARE?

JUST A CAPE?! ALL OF THE COOLEST SUPERHEROES WEAR CAPES!

"BATMAN. SUPERMAN.

"WONDER WOMAN ON FORMAL OCCASIONS.

"PLUS, THE CAPE DISTRACTS FROM THE FACT THAT I HAVE A REALLY WEIRD-LOOKING NECK."

YES!

I HAVE VANQUISHED THE GOLF GUARDIAN AND HAVE CONQUERED THIS HOLE!

NOW TO DESTROY *THIS* HOLE ON MY MARCH TO VICTORY!

WAIT, STARFIRE. THAT'S NOT HOW YOU PLAY MINI GOLF.

YOU'RE SUPPOSED TO TAP THE BALL INTO THE HOLE LIKE *THIS*.

I DO NOT UNDERSTAND...IF IT IS SO SIMPLE, THEN WHY HAVE THE BOYS BEEN ARGUING ALL DAY?

BECAUSE THEY MADE A BET. AND BETTING TURNS PEOPLE INTO IDIOTS...NOT THAT THEY WERE FAR OFF TO BEGIN WITH.

C'MON. MINI GOLF IS POINTLESS, ANYWAY. LET'S HIT THE ARCADE.

EDDIES'S ARCADE

I BELIEVE THE WINNER OF THE LAST HOLE GETS TO PLAY FIRST ON THE NEXT ONE...

SO, TIME TO TEE UP...

WHAT?!? HOW IS THIS AT ALL FAIR?

BEAST BOY'S JUST USING HIS NATURAL ABILITIES!

HE'S USING HIS TRUNK! IT'S THE SAME AS THROWING THE BALL!

OH, SO YOU WANT ME TO NOT USE ALL OF MY ABILITIES JUST TO MAKE IT MORE FAIR FOR YOU? I SEE HOW IT IS.

FINE. IF THAT'S HOW YOU WANT TO PLAY IT, LET'S DO IT.

OF COURSE.

YOU GOT IT! YOU GOT IT!

SPLAK

WHOOPS! I WAS JUST USING MY NATURAL ABILITIES AND I ACCIDENTALLY SPLIT YOUR GOLF BALL WITH MY BIRDARANG!

MY BAD.

TOTAL CHEAT MOVE, DUDE!

OH, SO IT'S NOT CHEATING WHEN YOU TURN INTO A GIANT ELEPHANT?

I CAN'T HELP THAT I CAN TURN INTO AN ELEPHANT!

I KNOW WHAT YOU CAN'T TURN INTO... THE WINNER OF THIS HOLE!

GUYS! WE DON'T WANT TO TURN THIS INTO A DEATH MATCH!

YES, WE DO!

HMM. MAYBE WE SHOULD REVISE THE BET...

THERE ARE SO MANY GAMES HERE, RAVEN. WHICH ONE ARE WE LOOKING FOR?

THIS IS IT.

OOOH! THE MACHINE OF CLAWS! WHAT IS THE OBJECTIVE OF THIS GAME?

YOU'RE SUPPOSED TO GET ONE OF THE DOLLS TO COME OUT OF THE MACHINE.

AND THERE WE GO. VICTORY COMPLETE.

BUT WHERE DOES THE CLAW COME IN?

BEATS ME.

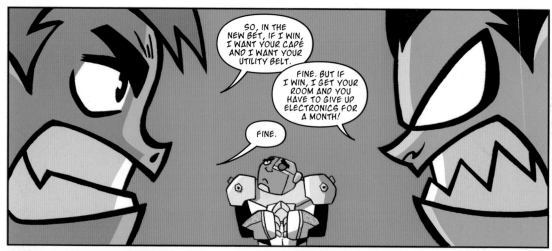

I WOULD LIKE TO ENTER THE CONTEST!

UNDER ONE CONDITION...IF I WIN, ALL FORMER BETS ARE NULL AND YOU TWO MUST GO BACK TO BEING FRIENDS!

... I'LL ALLOW IT.

TWEEET

WHAT?!

I AIN'T YOUR PUPPET, MAN!

OH, MAN! SO CLOSE!

BOOOOM

CREATORS

SHOLLY FISCH

Bitten by a radioactive typewriter, Sholly Fisch has spent the wee hours writing books, comics, TV scripts and online material for over 25 years. His comic book credits include more than 200 stories and features about characters such as Batman, Superman, Bugs Bunny, Daffy Duck, Spider-Man and Ben 10. Currently, he writes stories for Action Comics every month, plus stories for Looney Tunes and Scooby-Doo. By day, Sholly is a mild-mannered developmental psychologist who helps to create educational TV programmes, websites and other media for kids.

MERRILL HAGAN

Merrill Hagan is a writer who has worked on numerous episodes of the hit *Teen Titans Go!* TV show. In addition, he has written several *Teen Titans Go!* comic books and was a writer for the original *Teen Titans* series in 2003.

BEN BATES

Ben Bates is a comic book illustrator, colourist and writer. In addition to *Teen Titans Go!*, he has also worked on *Teenage Mutant Ninja Turtles*, *Mega Man*, *My Little Pony* and many other comics.

JORGE CORONA

Jorge Corona is a Venezuelan comic book artist who is well known for his all-ages fantasy-adventure series *Feathers* and his work on *Jim Henson's The Storyteller: Dragons*. In addition to *Teen Titans Go!*, he has also worked on *Batman Beyond*, *Justice League Beyond*, *We Are Robin*, *Goners* and many other comics.

GLOSSARY

accuse say that someone has done something wrong

birthright right or an object given to someone because the person is born into a specific family or group

compromise agree to something that is not exactly what either side wants in order to make a decision

confound cause surprise or confusion

conquer defeat and take control of an enemy

contraption strange or odd device or machine

demonic possession when someone is controlled by a demon or evil spirit

dingus funny word used in place of the name of something

dojo martial arts training place

flimflam nonsensical talk

guardian someone who carefully watches and protects something or someone

hankering hunger for something

infested filled with pests

kimono long, loose robe with wide sleeves and a sash

mutant something that has developed different characteristics from that of its original state

objective aim or goal that you are working towards

penetrate go inside or through something

renounce formally reject a belief, right or possession

restriction rule or limitation

technique method or way of doing something that requires skill

vanquish defeat or conquer an enemy in battle

witness person who has seen or heard something

VISUAL QUESTIONS & WRITING PROMPTS

1. Based on their facial expressions, what emotions or feelings are each Teen Titan experiencing in this panel?

2. At the end of the first story, Silkie changes after eating the pizza. Write a short story describing what happens next!

3. Why does Beast Boy turn into an elephant to play mini-golf? How do Cyborg and Robin feel about his transformation?

4. Why is Cyborg wearing this costume? What does it tell you about his role in the story?

READ THEM ALL!

TEEN TITANS GO!™